AGE OF DINOSAURS: **PTERODACTYL**

AGE OF DINOSAURS:

Pterodactyl

SHERYL PETERSON

CREATIVE EDUCATION

Published by Creative Education
P.O. Box 227, Mankato, Minnesota 56002
Creative Education is an imprint of The Creative Company
www.thecreativecompany.us

Design and production by Blue Design
Art direction by Rita Marshall
Printed by Corporate Graphics in the United States of America

Photographs by Alamy (Blickwinkel, Imagebroker, Interfoto, Pictorial Press Ltd), Bridgeman Art Library (English School), Corbis (Jonathan Blair), Dreamstime (Clearviewstock), Getty Images (DEA Picture Library, Ken Lucas), iStockphoto (Pete Karas), Library of Congress, Sarah Yakawonis/Blue Design

Library of Congress Cataloging-in-Publication Data
Peterson, Sheryl.
Pterodactyl / by Sheryl Peterson.
p. cm. — (Age of dinosaurs)
Summary: An introduction to the life and era of the flying contemporaries of dinosaurs known as pterodactyls, starting with the creatures' 1784 discovery and ending with present-day research topics.
Includes bibliographical references and index.
ISBN 978-1-58341-975-5
1. Pterodactyls—Juvenile literature. I. Title. II. Series.

QE862.P7P48 2010
567.918—dc22   2009025175

CPSIA: 120109 P01089

First Edition
9 8 7 6 5 4 3 2 1

CONTENTS

PTERODACTYL TALES

MYSTERIOUS FLYING REPTILE

Millions of years ago, the salty Jurassic seas covered much of the earth. In the shallow bottoms behind reefs, soft carbonate mud accumulated. Many creatures that fell into the mud or were washed into it from the ocean became stuck. As the mud hardened and turned into limestone, the bodies of horseshoe crabs, shrimps, and insects were eventually buried. Every so often, a small leather-winged creature would also become trapped, with the limestone perfectly preserving the details of its skeleton.

In 1784, workers in the Solnhofen rock quarry in Bavaria, a region of southern Germany, chiseled out slabs of limestone for roofing material. Cutting the stone with picks and small hoes was slow, difficult work, but chipping and scraping alongside the laborers was an Italian scientist named Cosimo Alessandro Collini. He was the **curator** of a private nature cabinet in the palace of Karl Theodor, Elector of Bavaria. (The "cabinet" was akin to today's natural history museums.) Collini patiently picked and dug and searched for signs of prehistoric animal life embedded in the rock. One day, while sweeping off a slab of dusty limestone, he discovered an imprint of a baffling, winged skeleton.

Was it a bat or a strange type of bird? Perhaps it was a miniature dragon! Collini was puzzled by the unusual skeleton preserved in the rock. The scientist did not recognize the specimen as a flying animal,

At the time the first pterosaur fossil was discovered, it was difficult to picture the type of animal that had left such an imprint behind.

so Collini wondered if it might be a mysterious sea creature instead. Since this animal was the first pterosaur to be discovered, Collini had nothing with which he could compare it.

Other scientists at the time thought the fossil belonged to an animal that was half-bird and half-bat. Little did they know that the newly discovered creature had lived 75 million years before birds and 150 million years before bats. The strange discovery was stored on a shelf in the nature cabinet in Mannheim, Germany, for nearly a quarter of a century.

During this time, the Napoleonic Wars were being fought across Europe. The French, led by General Napoleon Bonaparte (who later became emperor), were invading many countries in attempts to take control over as many governments as possible. To protect it from being stolen by plundering armies, Collini's raven-sized fossil was taken to Paris, France, in 1809. It was then delivered to the skilled French **anatomist** Baron Georges Cuvier for safekeeping and study.

Cuvier speculated that the bones came from a type of **reptile** and also noted that the creature's fourth finger was very long. He sketched a birdlike beast with a large head and batlike wing membranes that attached to a single, long finger on each side of the body and named the animal *Ptero-Dactyle,* or "winged-finger." By examining the animal's small teeth set in long jaws, Cuvier determined that it was neither bat nor bird but was more closely related to crocodiles than to any other living family. He called it a "flying reptile," yet that seemed incorrect to most people, since reptiles were usually limited

Baron Georges Cuvier

The man who named *Pterodactylus* possessed one of the finest scientific minds in history. Georges Cuvier was a French vertebrate zoologist and anatomist who is called the "Father of Paleontology." Cuvier was born in 1769 and became interested in the sciences at an early age. He revolutionized anatomy by developing a system of classifying animals into four groups based on their skeletal structure, and it was said that Cuvier could reconstruct a skeleton based on a single bone. A great scientific advancement occurred when Cuvier put forth his theories about extinction events. He believed that the earth was extremely old (but not as old as is now known), and that natural events such as catastrophic floods occurred, eliminating certain animal species forever. Cuvier believed that "animals have certain fixed and natural characters," and he determined that any similarities between organisms were due to common functions, not common ancestry. Still, the anatomist's new classification system brought scientists closer to understanding why animals have different structures. Cuvier's influence is commemorated in the names of many animals, including Cuvier's gazelle, Cuvier's toucan, and Cuvier's beaked whale.

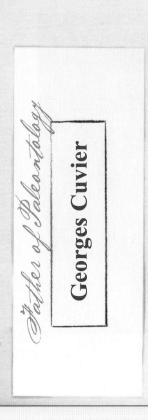

Father of Paleontology

Georges Cuvier

Solnhofen Treasures

Solnhofen is a town in southern Bavaria that gives its name to the limestone found in its vicinity, which began to form in the Jurassic Period, when the area was underwater. Because Solnhofen limestone is fine-grained and pure, it was often quarried for use in making roof and floor tiles from the late 1700s onward. Later, the stone was used in a kind of printing called lithography. Quarry workers were the first to discover fossilized remains that showed what life had been like both above and below the water level in that location millions of years ago. Fossils of pterodactyls, fish, turtles, jellyfish, and worms have been found, along with *Archaeopteryx*, the first primitive bird with feathered wings, and a tiny carnivorous dinosaur called *Compsognathus*. The only dinosaur found at Solnhofen, *Compsognathus* might have hunted for small reptiles and insects or perhaps a river carried its dead body to the lagoon, where it sank and became a fossil. The Bürgermeister Müller Museum, founded in Solnhofen in 1954, houses the quarry's large collection of treasures, including a plaster cast of *Archaeopteryx*.

to movement on the ground. Cuvier's term *Ptero-Dactyle* later took on the Latin form *Pterodactylus* and became the name for all similar **species** of pterosaur.

From then on, pterodactyl became the name commonly applied not only to the genus *Pterodactylus* but to all pterosaurs of the order Pterosauria. The group was known as "winged lizards," since over millions of years, they represented a class of reptiles called Sauropsida that lacked scales but possessed the ability to fly. The earliest pterosaurs appeared in the Late Triassic Period, about 220 million years ago, at approximately the same time as the first dinosaurs. They lived on through the Jurassic Period until the very end of the Cretaceous (about 65 million years ago).

From fossilized remains such as those found at Solnhofen (opposite), artists can render more lifelike images of prehistoric creatures (below).

It was not until 1817 that a second specimen of *Pterodactylus* was uncovered, once again from the Solnhofen quarries. Because these specimens were found in an area that had been a prehistoric sea, the idea that pterodactyls were water animals persisted among a small group of scientists as late as the 1830s. German zoologist Johann Georg Wagler even published an 1830 text on amphibians such as frogs and salamanders that showed a pterosaur using its wings as flippers.

Besides their wings, scientists noticed something else interesting about pterodactyls. Their bones had honeycombed air passages

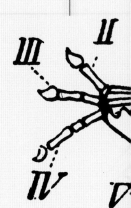

running through them, just like modern birds, which seemed to prove that the animals had been built for flight. Some paleontologists thought pterodactyls could fly to some extent but believed that they were not as capable as today's birds and bats. Others reasoned that the creatures were merely gliders.

In the late 1800s, a debate began between two leading British paleontologists, Richard Owen and Harry Seeley. They argued over whether pterodactyls were cold-blooded reptiles and poor fliers (as Owen believed) or warm-blooded primitive birds (as Seeley thought). The discovery of many more well-preserved pterodactyl fossils helped partially settle the matter. The creatures were proven to be reptiles and not related to birds. But the debate continued as to whether they were warm-blooded and if they had flown.

Since Collini and Cuvier first studied the earliest perplexing fossils, pterodactyl relatives have been found all over the world, from the North American *Pteranodon* to the Chinese *Dsungaripterus* to the South American *Quetzalcoatlus*. Thirty species of pterosaur have been found in the Solnhofen limestone alone. Yet even into the 21st century, pterosaurs continue to mystify scientists and the public.

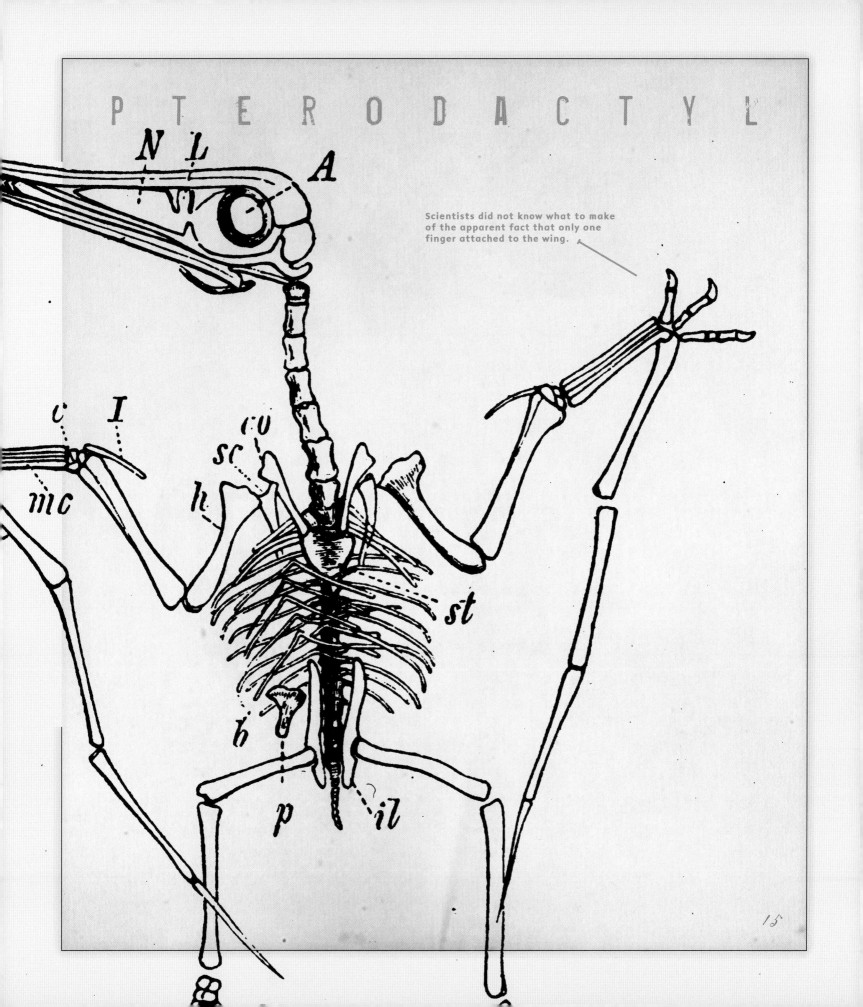

Scientists did not know what to make of the apparent fact that only one finger attached to the wing.

Giant *Quetzalcoatlus*

Quetzalcoatlus is the name of one of the largest flying creatures the world has ever known. This huge, winged North American creature was named after the Aztec feathered-serpent god Quetzalcoatl. Until the 1970s, scientists believed that *Pteranodon*, with its wingspan of up to 30 feet (9 m), was the biggest pterosaur. However, *Quetzalcoatlus*, discovered in 1971, had a wingspan of up to 40 feet (12 m). *Quetzalcoatlus* would have looked like a living aircraft. How could it have flown with such enormous wings? Scientists believe that it must have slowly and deliberately flapped its wings as many large seabirds do today. Once off the ground, it would have been able to soar like an albatross, barely beating its long, narrow wings as it flew over the ocean looking for fish. By the time the dinosaurs and most other prehistoric creatures went extinct about 65 million years ago, *Quetzalcoatlus* had been the only known pterosaur on Earth. Perhaps the gigantic pterosaurs had just gotten too big to live for very long, and as a species, they may have been victims of their own success.

WING-FINGERED FLIER

Dinosaurs may have ruled over the land for 160 million years, but pterodactyls and other winged reptiles ruled the prehistoric skies for just about as long. Some paleontologists say that pterodactyls had many similarities to dinosaurs. They point to such shared physical features as neck joints, jaw joints, small collarbones, and straight ankle hinges as proof.

Pterodactyls were strange creatures that flew over the earth during the Late Jurassic Period (appearing 150 to 145 million years ago) and were very different from flying creatures we know today. Some

Despite its large wingspan and seven-foot-long (2.1 m) legs, *Quetzalcoatlus* had a lightly built, hollow-boned body.

Between the
appearance of
Pterodactylus
(below) and that
of *Quetzalcoatlus*
(opposite) were
millions of years of
growth and change
in pterosaurs.

earlier reptiles had taken to the air before pterodactyls, but these were strictly gliders. Pterodactyls were probably the first **vertebrates** to achieve self-powered flight by flapping their wings. Some types of pterodactyls were small, about the size of a robin or a crow, with wingspans of only a few inches. Others were as large as today's vultures. Near the end of the Cretaceous Period, enormous relatives of the pterodactyls became common; some, such as *Ornithocheirus*, were as large as small airplanes!

Everything about the genus *Pterodactylus* was long, except for its short tail. It had long wings, a long slender neck, and an elongated head. In some cases, its head was as long as the rest of its body. *Pterodactylus* had long, narrow jaws with powerful muscles and a number of sharp, forward-facing teeth that were designed to grab prey, such as fish, and swallow them whole.

Since *Pterodactylus* was not a bird, it did not have feathers. However, it was covered with short, fine hair that may have provided insulation from the cold. *Pterodactylus* was a relatively small pterosaur, with adult wingspans ranging from 20 to 40 inches (50–102 cm). The animal's hollow bones did not contribute much to its overall weight of 2 to 10 pounds (.91–4.5 kg), enabling it to get off the ground and into the sky.

Until recently, some paleontologists had thought that pterodactyls hung upside

Strange Modern Sightings

For thousands of years, people around the world have reported pterodactyl sightings. The appearance of creatures thought to have been extinct for millions of years is an intriguing dilemma. In 1944, a U.S. pilot who was walking through a New Guinea jungle reported seeing a huge animal flying overhead. The man observed what he thought was a gigantic, dark gray bird with a wingspan that seemed to match his Piper airplane's. Giant flying reptiles have also been routinely sighted in Olympic National Park in the American state of Washington. In December 2007, a driver there told police that a pterodactyl caused him to run into a light pole. From the African Congo have come reports of a winged beast that residents call the Kongamoto, or "overwhelmer of boats." In 1925, a man was attacked by a creature and received wounds from its sharp beak. When natives were shown pictures of a pterodactyl, they said it was Kongamoto. Recently, there have been reports of prehistoric birdlike creatures near San Antonio, Texas, where *Quetzalcoatlus* once lived. It does make one wonder.

Could some have survived?

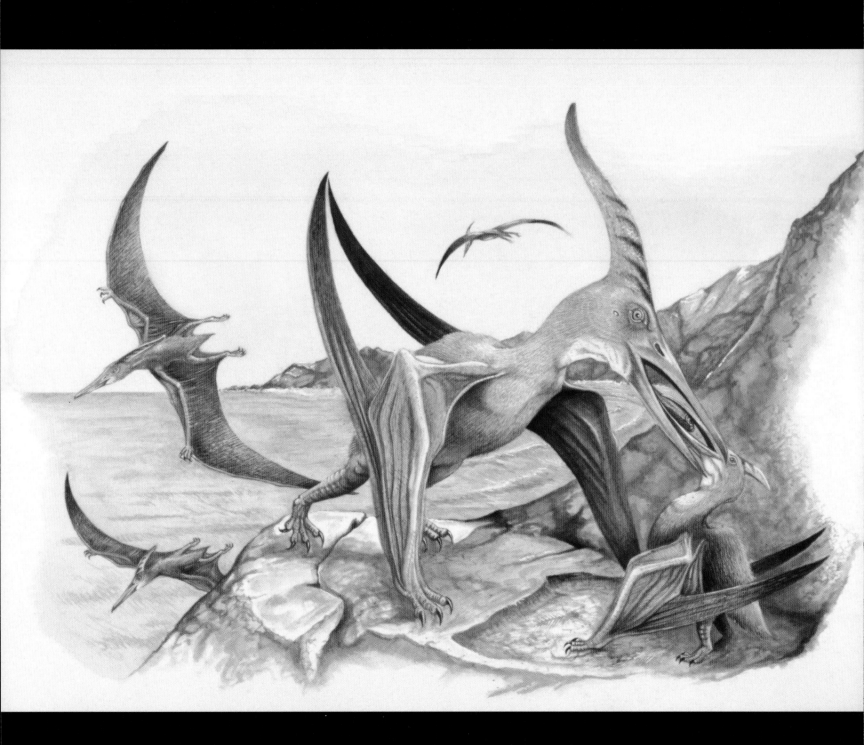

Its large, crested head set the Late Jurassic *Pteranodon* apart from other pterosaurs; this distinctively winged and toothless reptile was believed to have flown mainly by soaring.

down from trees like bats and would have needed to drop from a high place in order to gain enough momentum to begin flying. But now most scientists assert that pterodactyls moved around well on land and would have been able to attain flight from the ground.

The arm bones of *Pterodactylus* were long and lightweight. At the end of each arm were three short, clawed fingers and an extremely long fourth finger that reached all the way to the wing tip. This was known as the "wing finger." The wings of *Pterodactylus* were formed by a thin but tough, leathery skin that stretched between its body, the top of its legs, and its elongated fourth fingers. Although five toes were at the end of each leg, the fifth was too small to be of any use. *Pterodactylus* had a very short tail that did not assist in the animal's movement.

For its size, *Pterodactylus* had a relatively large brain inside its 2.4-inch-long (6 cm) skull. Shaped like a double-layered heart, its brain would be comparable to present-day birds of the same size, but it was more developed than other reptiles of similar size. Since flying is a complicated activity, *Pterodactylus* would have required a larger, more advanced brain to control its wings. Flying was the specialty of all pterodactyls, and they could travel much faster and farther than any of the land-based dinosaurs could.

Pterodactyls in general featured large eyes and probably had good vision. This means they would have been able to see across long distances as they flew over the land. Good eyesight would have come in

handy while searching for their next meal of fish and would have been
necessary to spot danger ahead.

Although pterodactyls and dinosaurs were closely related, they
were separate groups of animals. By definition, all dinosaurs moved
in an upright stance, while pterodactyls likely had a semi-upright
position when walking. While on land, smaller pterodactyls such
as *Rhamphorhynchus* and *Pterodactylus* probably moved rather
quickly on all four feet. Some pterodactyls such as *Dimorphodon* had
longer hind limbs and may have run on two hind legs like modern
roadrunners. Although some paleontologists think they could have
both walked and flown, pterodactyls were not the same as the birds
that lived during prehistoric times, nor were they like the birds we see
at our birdfeeders today.

Pterodactyls would have made their homes near a lake or sea, where
there was plenty of food available. The **carnivorous** pterodactyl ate
fish and other small animals. Flying over a body of water, a pterodactyl
would have dipped its beak and opened up its bottom jaw.
Scooping up water as it flew, the flying fisher would soon have
had a mouthful of tiny, tasty fish. Pterodactyls also dined
on **mollusks** and crabs and **scavenged** for dead animals
on land. If nothing else was available, a pterodactyl
would have dug its beak deep into the beach sand to
search for worms and insects.

It has been suggested that some pterosaurs
were able to swim much like modern
shorebirds. The recent discovery of unusual

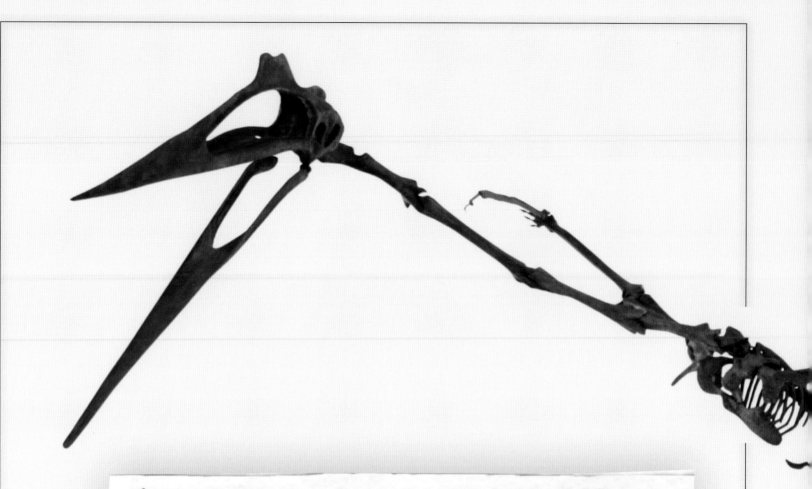

Tiny *Anurognathus*

A pterosaur smaller than a garden sparrow lived at the time of *Pterodactylus*. *Anurognathus*'s body was only about 3.5 inches (9 cm) long, but it had a wingspan of 20 inches (50 cm), or about 6 times its body length. *Anurognathus* means "without tail or jaw." The minute creature survived off of small flying insects such as lacewings and damselflies, catching them with its sturdy beak and needle-like teeth. Scientists speculate that *Anurognathus* lived near large sauropod dinosaurs such as *Diplodocus* and perched on their backs. They may have served a similar purpose as the present-day tick birds that sit on the backs of herd animals, feeding on the insects that the large animals attract. Being up high would have given *Anurognathus* some much-needed protection from predators below, and the bugs that constantly hovered around the skyscraper-sized dinosaurs would have provided a steady source of food. To date, only one fossil of the little creature is known. It was found in 1923 in the Solnhofen limestone quarries in Bavaria. *Anurognathus* is comparable in body size to a present-day hummingbird—but with much bigger, kite-shaped wings.

tracks in the American Southwest that show scrape marks were probably made by a pterodactyl paddling in shallow water. There is, however, no evidence of diving behavior.

Some scientists think pterodactyls had a throat pouch, much like a pelican's. Such a pouch could have been used for storing fish to transport back to a nesting area to feed its young. The baby pterodactyl would have put its beak in the adult's mouth and picked out its meal, piece by piece.

Pterodactyls would have been cautious when building a nest, because some dinosaurs were egg thieves. Two fossilized pterosaur eggs, reported to be about 121 million years old, were discovered in China in 2004. The eggs had a soft, leathery shell similar to that of crocodile and turtle eggs. This gave experts strong evidence that earlier pterodactyls also laid eggs. Since their bodies were not very big, they most likely laid only one or two eggs at a time. Females would not have been able to fly carrying more weight than that.

Another fossilized egg was found in Argentina in 2004. The egg and **embryo** inside it were among fossils of many juvenile and adult remains, suggesting that the winged reptiles lived in groups and protected their young. From what scientists can tell about the advanced development of the fossilized embryo, they reason that the young would have grown up fast and learned to fly quickly.

Some skeletal reconstructions show that early pterodactyls had shorter tails than their later counterparts, and their skulls were crestless.

25

PTEROSAURS AND DINOSAURS

The nonflowering ferns that continue to populate many forests today belong to a plant family that is approximately 360 million years old.

Pterosaurs were abundant during the Jurassic Period of 208 to 144 million years ago. At that time, the earth was a very different place. Scientists believe that most of Earth's landmasses, now called continents, were once a giant supercontinent called Pangaea. During the 64 million years of the Jurassic, the supercontinent broke into two major fragments—Laurasia in the north and Gondwana in the south. These fragments eventually separated into the seven continents that we know on Earth today. As the continents moved, they collided with pieces of the ocean floor, causing the formation of several mountain ranges around the world—including the Rocky Mountains in North America and the Alps in Europe.

As the landmasses shifted, sea levels rose, and **climates** changed in different parts of the world. Some tropical parts of the world became drier, while other places experienced periods of heavy monsoon rains. Flowering plants had not yet appeared on Earth during the Jurassic, but there were lush jungles full of **conifers**, **ginkgoes**, ferns, and stout, leafy **cycads**. The vast oceans became habitat for marine life forms such as sponges and corals.

Perhaps in response to this change in climate and abundance of food sources, some dinosaur species such as the **herbivores** *Diplodocus* and *Brachiosaurus* became gigantic in size. These dinosaurs were known as sauropods. Also roaming the planet were

Ocean Monster

Close under the ocean's surface lurked the sleek and sneaky *Metriorhynchus*, ready to attack. This marine crocodile of the Middle to Late Jurassic periods had a streamlined body with few of the scaly bumps and lumps that modern crocodiles possess. Measuring about 10 feet (3 m) long, the animal had a long, powerful tail that propelled it through the sea. Fossilized stomach contents show that *Metriorhynchus* (which means "moderate snout") snatched up anything that strayed too close to its mouth. The carnivorous sea monster tackled the giant fish *Leedsichthys* and successfully grabbed careless pterodactyls in mid-air by leaping out of the deep. Its paddle-like feet and finned tail made it so well suited to sea life that it came on land only to lay eggs. Then the huge animal would have returned to the sea immediately, leaving its young to hatch and make the perilous journey down the beach to the ocean alone. Ironically, hungry, flying reptiles such as pterodactyls may have been waiting in the air to dive down and pick up *Metriorhynchus*'s vulnerable offspring for their dinner.

smaller plant-eaters such as *Stegosaurus* and *Othnielia,* as well as giant meat-eaters such as *Allosaurus*. But there was more to Jurassic life than plants and dinosaurs. Creeping around in the dense foliage were a number of ratlike early **mammals**. In the seas were **plankton**, which in turn fed large fish such as *Leedsichthys*. Giant sea turtles weighing 4,500 pounds (2,041 kg) lived in the Jurassic ocean that covered what is now the state of Wyoming. The first marine crocodiles, such as *Metriorhynchus,* hunted in shallower oceans, along with the first sharklike animals. But *Metriorhynchus* also lurked near the water's surface and was capable of snatching *Pterodactylus* and other flying reptiles out of the air.

During the Late Jurassic, there were two major groups of pterosaurs living on Earth—*Pterodactylus* and *Rhamphorhynchus*. *Pterodactylus* had a very short tail but sported **cranial** ornamentation. *Rhamphorhynchus* was somewhat its opposite, with a long tail, no crest on the skull, and a slightly smaller size and wingspans ranging from 15 inches (38 cm) to 6 feet (1.8 m). *Rhamphorhynchus* used its long tail to balance itself during flight and was one of the last of the long-tailed pterosaurs to exist. At the start of the Cretaceous Period (approximately 144 million years ago), the pterosaurs all lost their tails and became exceedingly large.

Scientists generally agree that pterosaurs **evolved** from small, lizard-like creatures that climbed or lived in trees. Over time, these reptiles developed the ability to glide between trees by using the thin

Metriorhynchus **(opposite) likely preyed upon any low-flying pterosaurs, such as** *Rhamphorhynchus* **(above), that came within reach.**

29

flaps of skin that ran between their arms and legs as early wings. Eventually, pterodactyls swooped and dove across the Jurassic skies. They appeared in the fossil records as highly specialized fliers without any other species coming directly before them. Scientists have discovered pterodactyl fossils in places as far apart as France, Africa, and England, and have dug up specimens on every continent except Antarctica.

Fossils of the pterosaur *Germanodactylus* have been found in Germany and England. This specimen had strong finger claws, sharp teeth, and a wingspan of up to 40 inches (102 cm). Its name means "German finger." On top of its head was a distinctive bony crest. *Cycnorhamphus* was another pterosaur that shared the habitat of

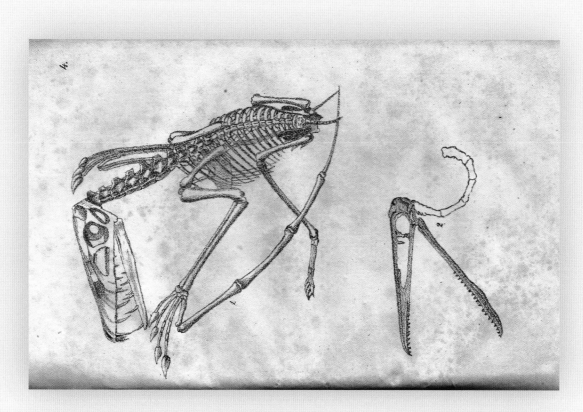

From early specimens documented by Georges Cuvier (opposite) to later findings on *Pteranodon* (pictured), scientists have pieced together pterosaur history.

While pterosaurs are often portrayed with disproportionately short legs, the head is just as often correctly downturned, showing its function in steering the reptile's flight.

Pterodactylus. It was given the name meaning "swan-like beak" by scientist Harry Seeley in 1870. A century later, paleontologists thought that a new species resembling *Cycnorhamphus* had been found and called it *Gallodactylus.* That name meant "Gallic finger" because it was first found in France (*Gallic* meaning "French"). In 1995, scientists realized that *Cycnorhamphus* and *Gallodactylus* were actually the same species, so the name reverted to *Cycnorhamphus.* This pterodactyl had a longer beak than most pterosaurs and had teeth only in the front of its long, slender jaws. Its wingspan was about five feet (1.4 m) long.

Another flying contemporary of *Pterodactylus* would have been *Ctenochasma*, or "comb jaw," which was discovered in 1852 in Germany. Its distinguishing feature was the more than 200 teeth that curved inward, resembling a comb. Most likely all of those teeth were used to filter out unwanted material when the creature fed on fish. *Ctenochasma* had a wingspan of about four feet (1.2 m).

As the Jurassic and Cretaceous periods progressed, flying creatures grew larger, and the smaller pterosaurs gradually died out. New species of the Cretaceous such as *Ornithocheirus* and *Pteranodon* were able to glide long distances, possibly even across continents. *Ornithocheirus* had a wingspan of up to 40 feet (12 m) and was first discovered in southern England in 1827. Most recently, a specimen was found in Brazil. *Pteranodon* was a lightweight, graceful pterodactyl that achieved a wingspan of 30 feet (9 m), and its fossils have been found all over North America, South America, Europe, and Asia. Small birds and flightless seabirds that had evolved in the Late Jurassic Period became more numerous throughout the Cretaceous as well.

And then, gradually, all of the flying reptiles and dinosaurs disappeared by about 65 million years ago during a mass **extinction** at the end of the Cretaceous. The cause of the mass extinction, known as the K-T (Cretaceous-Tertiary) extinction event, is still a matter of debate among scientists, but one possible explanation involves an increased amount of volcanic activity at that time.

Disagreements remain about many pterosaur features, such as whether the wings were attached to the entire body, including the tail (as shown opposite).

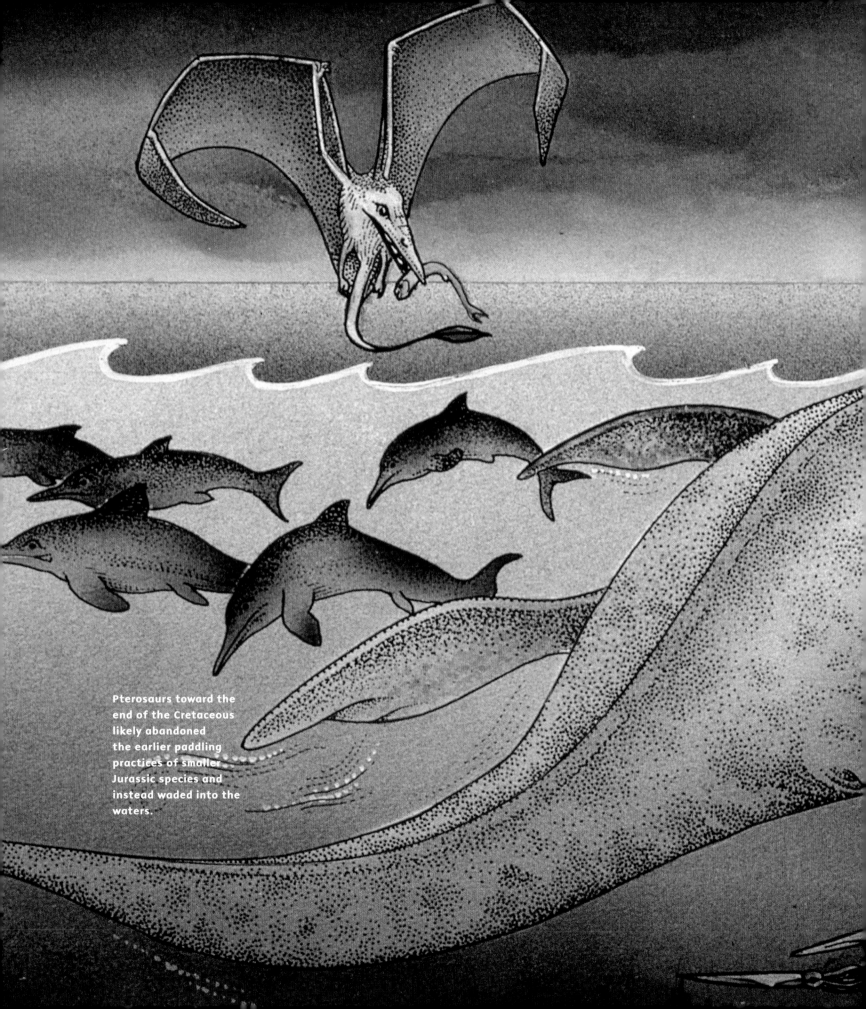

Pterosaurs toward the end of the Cretaceous likely abandoned the earlier paddling practices of smaller Jurassic species and instead waded into the waters.

The K-T event was most likely caused by an impact from outer space, though. A giant meteor that measured approximately six miles (9.7 km) across is known to have struck the planet near the coast of Mexico's Yucatán Peninsula around the same time that the dinosaurs disappeared. The impact likely released clouds of harmful gases and dust that filled the sky, blocking a significant amount of sunlight and resulting in a dramatic cooling effect that would have created months of freezing weather and darkness. (A similar series of events could also be attributed to the volcanic activity.) Many animals may not have been able to deal with such a change to their environment and would have weakened over time. With no plant material to eat, the herbivores would have died first. Without the plant-eaters available as prey, the meat-eaters, including pterosaurs, would have eventually starved to death themselves. Although exactly what happened may never be known, by the beginning of the Tertiary Period 65 million years ago, all of the pterosaurs had disappeared.

The Lost World

Pterodactyls became well known in 1912 when British author Sir Arthur Conan Doyle penned his popular book, *The Lost World*. Having already introduced readers to his famous detective, Sherlock Holmes, Doyle was ready to embark on a new adventure inspired by the discovery of dinosaur footprints in a quarry near his home in Sussex, England. Doyle wondered what a place where pterodactyls and dinosaurs had survived from prehistoric times would be like. The book's main character, Professor Challenger, leads a group of explorers into the swamps of Venezuela to find the beasts he has heard about. When Challenger encounters pterodactyls, he reports, "It was a wonderful sight to see at least a hundred creatures of such enormous size and hideous appearance all swooping like swallows with swift, shearing wing-strokes above us." To add to the drama of the novel, the pterodactyls attack the group. Luckily, the explorers escape and return to camp. Soon after, the team witnesses a war between early humans and a vicious tribe of apelike creatures. Almost 80 years later, American author Michael Crichton put a modern spin on Doyle's subject when he wrote *Jurassic Park*.

FROM UGLY TO ELEGANT

For most of the past two centuries, pterodactyls have been portrayed as ugly, flying fiends with dark, leathery skin. They were thought to have been part bat, part bird, and part crocodile. The nightmarish creatures were also disparaged by early scholars as flying failures. The first scientists to study pterodactyls did not believe that the animals could have flown because their wings weren't stiff enough to be able to flap. Also, one finger did not seem enough to support the wings, especially when compared with the four fingers that bats use to stretch out their wings.

Nineteenth-century scientists also believed that the pterodactyl was accident-prone. Its wings, they said, were as thin as a rubber band and likely could have snagged easily on tree branches or jagged rocks. Many paleontologists agreed that the pterodactyl was a clumsy creature that was unsteady on its feet and, if it could fly at all, could fly only when the wind was just right. They theorized that pterodactyls survived only because they had no direct competition until the first birds appeared.

In Sir Arthur Conan Doyle's 1912 book *The Lost World,* pterodactyls are portrayed as hideous aerial scavengers that drip poisonous drool as they swoop down to bite at a group of humans. A pterodactyl in the 1933 movie *King Kong* was given much the same treatment, as the black creature with reptilian wings lunged at the leading female

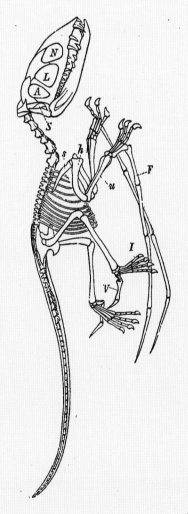

In *King Kong*, the giant gorilla lived on a tropical island that was home to prehistoric and other abnormal creatures such as the pterodactyl.

character with its monstrous hind claws. In the 1960s and early '70s, most museum displays and textbooks still presented pterodactyls as creepy creatures with batlike skin.

Later in the 1970s, though, new fossils and fresh studies of old specimens began to upgrade the pterodactyl's image. Scientists examined the preserved wing membranes that came from the same Bavarian quarry in which the first pterosaur specimen had been found. They discovered that the wing membranes had not been weak at all. Long, stiff fibers of connective tissue called ligaments had stretched across the wing and were probably attached to muscles that controlled the tension of the wing's surface. Pterodactyl wings were strong appendages that could flap powerfully and lift the creature upward to soar high and fast. The creatures were more active fliers than most modern birds, in fact, with the exceptions of such species as swifts and hummingbirds.

Although some scientists still debate the pterodactyl's flying ability, most believe that it was an extraordinary, elegant beast. In fact, the pterodactyl was one of the best-equipped fliers of prehistoric times. If it was on the ground and wanted to fly away, it would have faced the wind and spread its wings. All pterosaurs had a shoulder joint socket that pointed backward instead of forward, similar to a bird's, allowing them to flap their wings.

Pterodactyls would have been better climbers than walkers while on land. No one knows for sure how a pterodactyl moved on the ground, but some scientists think that it walked on its back legs. Others think it would have scuffled along on all fours. Most agree that it would have had a slow and difficult time getting anywhere on the ground. However, it would have been able to move around more easily than a bat, which can only crawl along on its stomach.

Scientists are still learning about the physical makeup and behavior of pterodactyls. Today, most believe that pterosaurs in general were warm-blooded. Active flight is a strenuous activity, and any creature that flew would have needed to have a high **metabolism** such as that possessed by modern warm-blooded animals. Another indication that pterodactyls might have been warm-blooded is that they had mammal-like hearts. Such hearts have four chambers and are designed to pump blood efficiently to all parts of the body to help sustain movement. Cold-blooded animals such as reptiles have a three-chambered heart that works faster in warmer temperatures but is not as efficient.

In 1998, a new pterodactyl specimen named *Pterodactylus kochi* was found that shed light on the creature's appearance. The specimen had a soft-tissue crest on the skull, which would have been a colorful display to attract females. The fossil showed unusually long, sharp claws and hairlike strands running down the back of the pterodactyl's neck. The feet showed evidence of webbing between the toes, like a duck's foot.

The Art of Flight

At the beginning of the 1900s, people all around the world were fascinated with flying. Orville and Wilbur Wright (pictured) had just taken their first flight in an airplane at Kitty Hawk, North Carolina, in 1903, and the interest carried over, even to the study of pterodactyls. Engineers and inventors of the 20th century regarded flight as the greatest achievement in the art of movement. They studied bats and birds in their attempts to build the first flying machine for humans. They also analyzed the lightly built skeleton, strong muscles, and wide wings of the pterodactyl. Scientists today at Texas Tech University are studying pterodactyls' bodies to design a new spy plane called the Pterodrone. Pterodactyls went extinct millions of years ago, but the newly designed plane will bring the flying reptiles to life, replacing blood and bones with carbon fiber and batteries. The unmanned, robotic spy plane is about the size of a crow, with a similar wingspan of nearly 32 inches (81 cm). It is designed to fly, sail, and land in hard-to-reach places to gather information.

Ten years later, in February 2008, a Brazilian research team led by paleontologist Alexander Kellner discovered a tiny pterosaur specimen in northeastern China that was the size of a sparrow. Named *Nemicolopterus crypticus*, which means "hidden flying forest dweller," the tree-dwelling pterosaur most likely fed on insects and shows the closest link between pterosaurs and birds. It had long, curved toes like a bird but the reptilian wings and bone structure of a pterosaur. Still, Kellner was careful to point out that, although pterosaurs and birds may "share a common ancestor, . . . each one went along a different evolutionary path."

From the feathered *Archaeopteryx* to the long-tailed *Rhamphorhynchus* and short-tailed *Pterodactylus*, ancient fliers underwent startling evolutions.

To discover that path, paleontologists continue to search for fossils of the flying reptiles at sites such as Brazil's Araripe Plateau, China's Xinjiang region, and the Qaratai Mountains of Kazakhstan. The world first learned about the prehistoric pterodactyls because of the efforts of scientists such as Collini and Cuvier. Building upon the discoveries made in the last century, scientists of today can make advanced skeletal reconstructions of pterodactyls, further study their biology, and more accurately analyze the structure of their wings.

Any time scientists learn something new about pterodactyls or other prehistoric creatures, they come closer to understanding what life on Earth was like millions of years ago. More than 200 years after the first pterosaur fossil was discovered, scientists are still learning more about them and their reptilian relatives. And two centuries from now, they will probably have still more to discover.

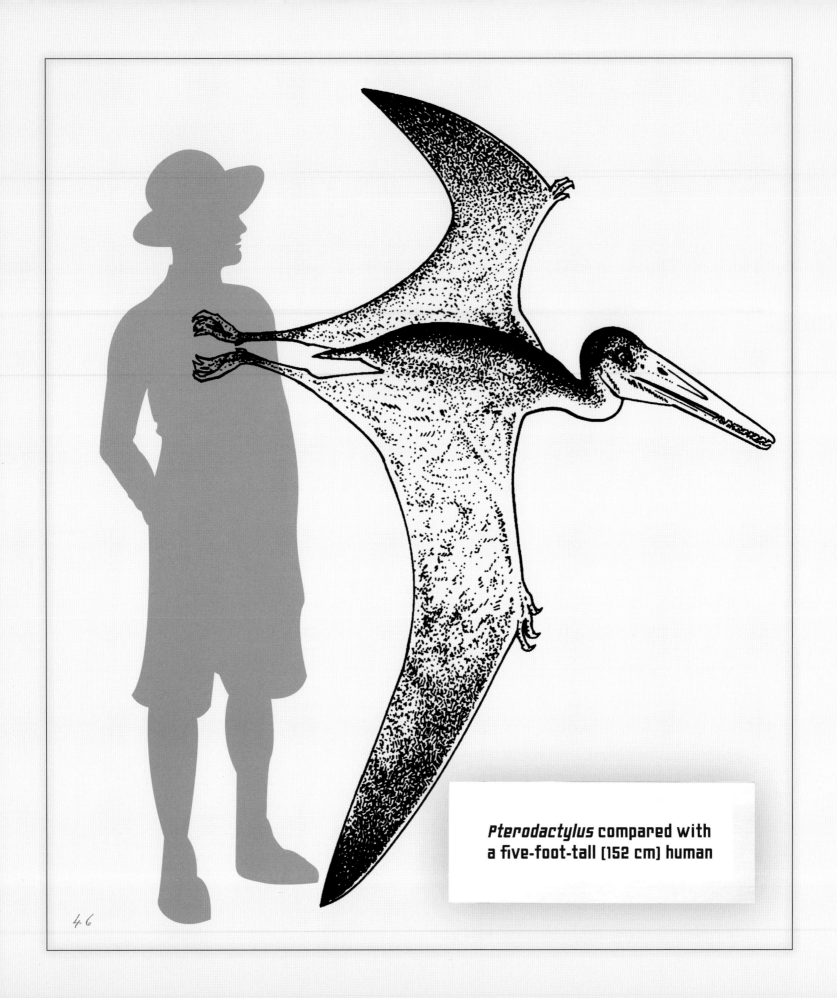

Pterodactylus compared with a five-foot-tall (152 cm) human

46

GLOSSARY

anatomist—an expert in anatomy, or the structure of an animal or plant

carnivorous—describing an animal that feeds on other animals

climates—the long-term weather conditions of areas

conifers—evergreen trees, such as pines and firs, that bear cones

cranial—relating to the skull or cranium

curator—the person in charge of a museum or art collection

cycads—tropical palmlike plants that bear large cones

embryo—an organism in the early stages of development before it emerges from the egg

evolved—adapted or changed over time to survive in a certain environment

extinction—the act or process of becoming extinct; coming to an end or dying out

ginkgoes—large ornamental trees with fan-shaped leaves, fleshy fruit, and edible nuts

herbivores—animals that feed only on plants

mammals—warm-blooded animals that have a backbone and hair or fur, give birth to live young, and produce milk to feed their young

metabolism—the processes that keep a body alive, including making use of food for energy

mollusks—a large group of soft-bodied invertebrates that includes snails, clams, and octopuses

paleontology—the study of fossilized plants and animals

plankton—the small or microscopic animal and plant organisms that float or drift in the water

reptile—a cold-blooded animal with scaly skin that typically lays eggs on land

scavenged—to have gathered and eaten the rotting flesh of animals found dead

species—a group of living organisms that share similar characteristics and can mate with one another

vertebrates—animals that have a backbone, or spinal column

SELECTED BIBLIOGRAPHY

Bakker, Robert. *The Dinosaur Heresies: New Theories Unlocking the Mystery of the Dinosaurs and Their Extinction.* New York: Morrow, 1986.

Buffetaut, Eric, and Jean-Michel Mazin. *Evolution and Paleobiology of Pterosaurs.* London: Geological Society of London, 2003.

Fastovsky, David, and David Weishampel. *The Evolution and Extinction of the Dinosaurs.* Cambridge: Cambridge University Press, 2005.

Haines, Tim, and Paul Chambers. *The Complete Guide to Prehistoric Life.* Buffalo, N.Y.: Firefly Books, 2007.

Malam, John, and John Woodward. *Dinosaur Atlas.* New York: DK Publishing, 2006.

Rogers, Dr. Kristina Curry, (vertebrate paleontologist, Macalester College, St. Paul, MN). Online interview, December 12, 2008.

INDEX

READ MORE

Bennett, S. Christopher. *Pterosaurs: The Flying Reptiles*. New York: Franklin Watts, 1995.

Ellis, Richard. *Sea Dragons: Predators of the Prehistoric Oceans*. Lawrence, Kans.: University Press of Kansas, 2005.

Lambert, David. *The Ultimate Dinosaur Book*. New York: DK Publishing, 1993.

Wellnhofer, Peter. *The Illustrated Encyclopedia of Pterosaurs*. London: Salamander Books, 1991.

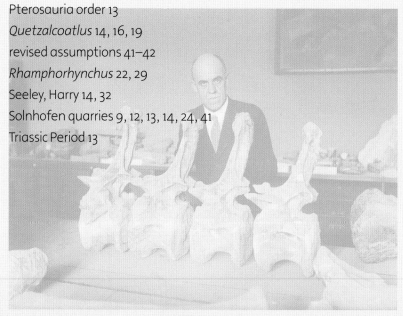